Samuel Estwick

Considerations on the Negroe Cause Commonly so Called,

addressed to the Right Honourable Lord Mansfield, Lord Chief Justice of

the Court of King's Bench, &c.

Samuel Estwick

Considerations on the Negroe Cause Commonly so Called,
addressed to the Right Honourable Lord Mansfield, Lord Chief Justice of the Court of King's Bench, &c.

ISBN/EAN: 9783337411039

Printed in Europe, USA, Canada, Australia, Japan

Cover: Foto ©Andreas Hilbeck / pixelio.de

More available books at **www.hansebooks.com**

CONSIDERATIONS

ON THE

NEGROE CAUSE

COMMONLY SO CALLED,

ADDRESSED TO

THE RIGHT HONOURABLE

LORD MANSFIELD,

LORD CHIEF JUSTICE of the COURT of
KING'S BENCH, &c.

By SAMUEL ESTWICK, A. M. LL.D.
Member of Parliament for the Borough of *Weſtbury*.

THE THIRD EDITION.

LONDON:
Printed for J. DODSLEY, in PALL-MALL.
M.DCC.LXXXVIII.

[Price 2 *s.*]

ADVERTISEMENT

TO THE

READER.

THE judgment that was given in the cafe of Somerfet and Knowles, fo contrary to the received opinions at that time, and to the general fenfe of the nation before, having laid the foundation upon which all the various fpeculations that upon this fubject have fince been raifed, and which are at length fo magnified and enlarged as to become the object of a Parliamentary Inquiry; it is imagined, that a review of fome of the arguments which were made ufe of on that occafion may not, in the prefent moment, be thought either impertinent or unfeafonable.

It is under this idea then, that the following Confiderations are again brought forward to the public notice: and although

their

their primary object was to fix and ascertain the ground upon which the Owner claimed a right to his Negroe, and insomuch to develope the subject from the mist and mystery with which it was want to be surrounded; yet in the course of their perusal it will, perhaps, be found, that there are not wanting answers to some of the most leading and popular objections of the day; that there are some observations and remarks, as new in themselves, as they have been and are still unanswered; and withal, that no part of the performance is of a complexion that can do injury, that may not produce some good, and of which the author, notwithstanding the distance of time from its publication, feels that he has either cause to be ashamed, or reason to repent.

PREFACE.

THE firſt Edition of the following Conſiderations on the Negroe Cauſe was written with haſte, and publiſhed in a hurry. The hope of ſeeing ſome much abler pen than mine engaged in the diſcuſſion of ſo important a queſtion, and yet ſeemingly ſo little underſtood, withheld me from the undertaking; till diſappointment made it the reſolution of an hour, and want of time the effect of a few days attention only. It was evident that whatever was to have been ſuggeſted on the ſubject, ought to have been known antecedently to the legal deciſion of the Caſe: but led on by the expectation of the more

uſeful

useful endeavours of others, already was the Term, in which judgment was to be given, treading closely on my heels, without my having taken one single step in advance of the design. Thus circumstanced, such dispatch became necessary as could not fail to produce errors, imputable both to me and the printer. Whilst one part of the pamphlet was printing, the other was preparing for the press : but even this expedition had not its desired effect. The Judgment was beforehand with the Publication : whereby the Considerations themselves were deprived of their object, and I, in some measure, foiled in my purpose. Upon finding however that the very grounds of my argument (to wit, the opinions of the Lord Chancellors Hardwick and Talbot) were the subjects of *due attention* to the Court, and that the determination rested on this particular Case *only*, from circumstances of insufficiency arising out of the return made to the writ of Habeas Corpus, I was induced to suffer

this

this performance to make its appearance to the public eye, though, like Hamlet's Ghoft, with all its imperfections on its head.

But being now called upon for a fecond Edition, I have carefully corrected the errors of the firft, fo far as they were perceiveable to me. I have confiderably enlarged the work itfelf. I have inferted feveral notes, in fome of which the principles of the late publifhed argument of Mr. Hargrave, and the argument itfelf, as applied to the merits of this queftion, are *fhortly* examined, though (with what is offered in the text) it is to be prefumed, *fully* refuted.

Suppofing too, that the judgment of the Court of King's Bench in this cafe might be no improper addition, I have, from the moft authentic copy I was able to procure, inferted it here : taking the liberty at the fame time of making fome few occafional remarks upon it.

The following *is faid* to be the fubftance of Lord Mansfield's fpeech in the cafe of Somerfet and Knowles : " We pay due at-

tention

tention to the opinion of Sir Philip Yorke
and Mr. Talbot in the year 1729, by which
they *pledged* themfelves to the Britifh Planters for the legal confequences of bringing
Negroe-flaves into this kingdom, or their
being baptized;"which opinion was repeated
and recognized by Lord Hardwick, fitting
as Chancellour, on the 19th of October 1749,
to the following effect: He faid, "that Trover
would lay for a Negroe-flave: that a notion
prevailed, that if a flave came into England,
or became a Chriftian, he thereby became
emancipated; but there was no foundation
in law for fuch a notion : that when he and
Lord Talbot were Attorney and Solicitor
General, this notion of a flave becoming
free by being baptized prevailed fo ftrongly,
that the Planters induftrioufly prevented
their becoming Chriftians : upon which
their opinion was taken; *and upon their
beft confideration they were both clearly of opinion*, that a flave did not in the leaft alter
his fituation or ftate towards his Mafter
or *Owner*, either by being chriftened, or

coming

coming to England: that though the ftatute of Charles II. had abolifhed Tenure fo far, that no man could be a *Villein regardant*; yet if he would acknowledge himfelf a *Vellein* engroffed in any Court of Record, he knew of no way by which he could be entitled to his freedom, without the confent of his Mafter." We feel the force of the inconveniences and confequences that will follow the decifion of this queftion : yet all of us are fo clearly of one opinion upon the *only* queftion before us, that we think we ought to give judgment without adjourning the matter to be argued before all the judges, as ufual in the Habeas Corpus, and as we at firft intimated an intention of doing in this cafe. The only queftion then is, *Is the Caufe returned fufficient for the remanding him ? If not*, he muft be difcharged. The Caufe returned is, the *flave* abfented himfelf and departed from his mafter's fervice, and refufed to return and ferve him during his ftay in England ; whereupon, by his mafter's orders, he was put on board the

B   fhip

fhip by force, and there detained in fecure cuftody, to be carried out of the kingdom and fold. So high an act of dominion muft derive its authority, if any fuch it has, from the law of the kingdom *where* executed. A foreigner cannot be imprifoned *here* on the authority of any law exifting in his own country. The power of a mafter over his fervant is different in all countries, more or lefs limited or extenfive; the exercife of it therefore muft always be regulated by the laws of the place where exercifed. The ftate of flavery is of fuch a nature, that it is incapable of being now introduced by Courts of Juftice upon mere reafoning, or inferences from any principles natural or political; it muft take its rife from pofitive law; the origin of it can in no country or age be traced back to any other fource. Immemorial ufage preferves the memory of pofitive law long after all traces of the occafion, reafon, authority, and time of its introduction, are loft; and in a Cafe fo odious as the condition of flaves

muft

muſt be, taken ſtrictly, the power claimed
by this return was never in uſe here : no
maſter ever was allowed here to take a
ſlave by force to be ſold abroad becauſe he
had deſerted from his ſervice, or for any
other reaſon whatever ; we cannot ſay,
the Cauſe ſet forth by this return is allowed or approved of by the laws of this
kingdom, and therefore the man muſt be
diſcharged."

I muſt confeſs, I have been greatly puzzled in endeavouring to reconcile this
judgment with this ſtate of it, and with
my comprehenſion.

" We pay due attention to the opinion
of Sir Philip York and Mr. Talbot," are
the words of the Noble Lord who delivered the judgment of the Court; and yet the
judgment is, in operation and effect, direct-
ly ſubverſive of the opinion. Now I muſt
take for granted that this opinion would
not have been cited, eſpecially in ſo affir-
mative a manner, if it had had nothing at

all

all to do with the Cafe then before the
Court: becaufe fuch citation would have
been unmeaning and unneceffary. This
being admitted, it follows, that the law
laid down in this opinion was either the
law of the Cafe, or it was not. If it were
the law of the Cafe, the judgment would
have been governed by that law, and confequently contrary to what it is. If it
were not the law of the Cafe, in order to
fhew what the law is, and that the law and
the judgment might correfpond with each
other, as caufe and effect, it would feem,
ex neceffitate rei, that the doctrine advanced
in this opinion fhould have been fet afide by
the fuperior force of legal argumentation
and authority. But the reafoning upon the
judgment ftands thus : In the Premifes
this opinion is cited as authority ; then,
without any middle term denying that
authority, the conclufion is, by the judgment, that it is no authority at all. Under
thefe problematical circumftances the only
folution

folution poffible to me was, that there might be two decifions intentionally contained under one judgment: that is to fay, that the opinion of Sir Philip York and Mr. Talbot, was the law upon the general merits of the queftion ; and that this judgment of the Court was the law upon this particular ftate of it. Thus for inftance : if the return made to the writ of Habeas Corpus in this Cafe had denied the lawfulnefs of the writ itfelf, and Mr. Steuart had claimed Somerfet upon the ground only of being his commercial *property*; then the opinion of Sir Philip York and Mr. Talbot had operated as law and authority : but as the return had admitted the right of flavery, and Mr. Steuart had claimed Somerfet as his flave, there being no laws of flavery now *in ufe* in this country, either for Negroes, or for any other fpecies of the human being, the judgment of the court was, *from the infufficiency of the Caufe returned*, the law of this Cafe.

But

But no fooner had this reconciliation taken place in. my mind, than another perplexity followed. In the recital of the opinion recognized by Lord Hardwick, fitting as Chancellour, it is made to conclude thus : " that though the Statute of Charles II. had abolifhed Tenure fo far that no man could be a *Villein regardant*, yet if he would acknowledge himfelf a Villein ingroffed in any Court of Record, he knew of no way by which he could be entitled to his freedom without the confent of his Mafter."

Now, by connecting this latter with the former part of the opinion, in the manner it is done, it appears, as if Lord Hardwick meant to declare, that the ftate or fituation of Negroes towards their mafters or owners arofe out of, and was founded upon, the remains of the antient laws of villenage in this country. That Lord Hardwick might have faid what is here ftated, in order to fhew (by way of illuftration of the Cafe upon which he was

then

then arguing) that even an Englifhman might ftill become a flave in this country, *if he pleafed*, I cannot deny: but with any intention to prove that the condition of Negroes proceeded from, and was the fame with, the condition of villeins, is, I muft affert, either the miftake of the perfon from whofe notes this fpeech was taken, or the intention of him to puzzle and perplex the Cafe: for it is manifeftly impoffible that the Court could have put fo much felf-contradiction and ignorance of the law in the mouth of fo wife and fo great a lawyer. His Lordfhip fays, " that Trover will lie for a Negroe flave." Now, can any thing be more expreffive of the law and condition of Negroes than this is ? What the nature of an action of Trover is, and what kind of property is required in a plaintiff to maintain fuch an action, every Tyro of the law muft be acquainted with. Would his Lordfhip have faid, that Trover would lie for a villein ? Every Tyro of the law knows that it would not.

But

But if a Negroe and a villein were governed by the fame laws, Trover would lie for a villein. His Lordfhip's own words therefore, and not this combination of them, are the beft comment upon his meaning ; and he in me, *non tali auxilio eget*, &c. It is enough that I have given the clew ; the reader will unravel the reft himfelf.

I have now only a fhort word or two more to add, in addrefs to the reader ; relying, from my own confcioufnefs, upon his candour, that whatever errors of the head he may difcover, he will impute nothing that is wrong to the dictates of my heart. It is not the want of humanity, it is not the want of feeling, but the poffeffion of both, with the love of truth, that has given birth to thefe Confiderations. My motives have been, to fhew that America does not afford that fcene of barbarity, which mifreprefentation would have painted upon it : that cruelties and diftrefs are to be found in much greater excefs even in this *elyfium* of liberty : that whatever is the ftate and condition of Negroes, it is Great Britain and

not

not America that is refponfible for it: that this therefore is a Britifh, and not an American queftion; as well it might be, fince, if I may be allowed to reafon chymically upon the occafion, whatever property America may have in its drugs, it is Great Britain that receives the effential oyl extracted from them. Thefe have been my views. I neither meant to condemn or approve the ftate and condition of Negroes. I have appealed to the law: if the traffic made of them be as agreeable to right reafon as it is according to law, I am glad of it; if it be not, let ftate neceffities juftify ftate tricks. But I meant an apology for, and not a panegyrick upon, myfelf.

C

CONSIDERATIONS

ON THE

NEGROE CAUSE, &c.

MY LORD,

BEING, both by birth and fortune, connected with one of the Iflands in America, I was led, fomewhat intereftedly as your Lordfhip may fuppofe, to attend to the arguments that were lately offered in the Court of King's Bench, in the Cafe of Somerfet the Negroe *verfus* Knowles and others. It was a new cafe, faid to be full of concern to America; and it had engroffed much of general expectation. My object therefore was that of information : but, without meaning to leffen the labours, or

depreciate

depreciate the merits of the learned counfel concerned therein, I muft confefs, that the lights thrown on the cafe did by no means appear to me as, on either fide, de-cifive of the point in queftion [a]. It is true that a vaft and extenfive variety of reading was fhewn and difcovered: the profoundeft depths of learning and fcience were fa-thomed and explored : lawgivers, philofo-phers, civilians, from all hiftoric exiftence, were brought to light and examined : the examples,

[a] The late publication of Mr. Hargrave's argu-ment, as one of Somerfet's counfel, gives me the fatisfaction of feeing in the whole, what I had before the opportunity of hearing only in part. I confefs I know not which moft to admire, the labour of this Gentleman's refearches, or the ingenuity with which his collected materials are fyftematized and difpofed. It is a hiftory, perhaps the moft compleat that is, of the rife, progrefs, decline, and general ftate of Slavery ; and, whilft it does as much honour to his humanity as to his underftanding, will ferve as a light to en-lighten the footfteps of pofterity, fhould a revival of the laws of Villenage be ever attempted in this coun-try : but, having faid this, I muft recur to my former opinion, that, learned as his arguments are in general, in this particular cafe they are founded on falfe and

miftaken

examples, definitions, and opinions, which Mofes, Ariftotle, Juftinian, Grotius, Pufendorff, and the reft, had given of flavery, were cited, explained, and enlarged upon : the edicts and regulations of French, Spanifh, German, Flemifh, and Dutch police on this head were mentioned and produced.

miftaken principles, and are totally inapplicable to the merits of the prefent queftion. His firft principle or point is, (vid. p. 12.) that " whatever Mr. Steuart's Right may be, it fprings out of the condition of flavery ; and accordingly, fays he, the return *fairly* admits flavery to be the *fole* foundation of Mr. Steuart's Claim." Thus, with a *Petitio Principii*, which neither is, can, or will be admitted, and upon a manifeft error in the return made to the writ of Habeas Corpus, does the argument of Mr. Hargrave commence, reft, and depend. But if, inftead of admitting, there being no law to countenance fuch admiffion, the return had relinquifhed the right, and denied the claim, of flavery : if it had fet forth, that Mr. Steuart was the *bona fide* purchafer of Somerfet in the legal courfe of trade : that he had bought him out of a fhip's cargoe from Africa, together with fome elephants teeth, wax, leather, and other commodities of that country, for which he paid his money, or otherwife gave in exchange the manufactures of this country : that he had brought him here as an article of commerce with his other goods, under the fanction of the

ed. But, my Lord, with all due deference
and fubmiffion, may I afk, how applicable
was this antiquated and foreign doctrine to
the cafe then under your Lordfhip's con-
templation ? The politics of Ariftotle are
not the rules of the Court of King's Bench;
neither is Roman jurifprudence the law of
that court. As a difplay of general know-

the laws of trade : that he meant to export him hence
under the fame protection, with his other property, in
order to be fold for his better advantage in one of the
Englifh Colonies in America : that a writ of *Habeas*
Corpus might as well iffue on account of his elephants
teeth, his wax, his leather, and his other commodities
of that country, as on account of his Negroe, they being exprefsly under the fame predicament of law, and
fo forth : I fay, under fuch circumftances, and upon
fuch a return, what would have become of this ftately
pile of elaborate argument ?

High-built, like Babel's tower, to magnify the fall !
Muft not the lawyers have faught new ground to build
upon ? Muft not the Court have loft that error of infufficiency, which now fupports its only right of Judgment ?

Note, Although this argument of Mr. Hargrave is faid
to have been delivered in the particular Cafe of Somerfet
a Negroe, yet it is meant and intended as a courfe of
reafoning upon the general queftion of the ftate and
condition *of Negroes.*

ledge,

ledge, it had with me, as it muſt have had
with every one preſent, its great abundance
of merit and commendation; and I had
followed the learned gentlemen, with the
higheſt pleaſure, in their travels and pur-
ſuits abroad in ſearch of matter of illuſtra-
tion, if the caſe had been brought home
with them at laſt, and reſted on its own
native ground and foundation. But herein,
my Lord, I found myſelf unſatisfied and
diſappointed: for how the queſtion remain-
ed with your Lordſhip as a point of law for
the judgment of the Court, I own, I was
unable to comprehend, or to learn. It is
therefore, my Lord, that I now take the
liberty to offer the following Conſiderations
to your Lordſhip's notice and obſervance;
truſting to the importance of the ſubject,
and to your wonted candour, for my apology and pardon in the attempt.

I have read, my Lord, to diſtinguiſh,
and have been ever taught to know, that
the Lord Chief Juſtice of the Court of
King's Bench is the great and firſt expoun-
der

der of the laws of this Realm; great and firſt in dignity and in office; in your Lordſhip's perſon, great and firſt profeſſedly in capacity alſo. Of theſe laws then, my Lord, I have apprehended that there are but two · kinds, however ſub-divided into ſorts or ſpecies: the unwritten, or common law, of which judicial deciſions are the evidence: or the written or ſtatute law, otherwiſe called acts ´of parliament. Now, my Lord, ſo far as this caſe is referrable to either of theſe eſtabliſhments, ſo far it lies before the Court, and falls under the cognizance of your Lordſhip. This is the ſource of enquiry leading to your judgment and determination; and all without the circle of this, I conceive to be inappoſite and eccentric. The firſt queſtion then, that would ſeem to ariſe on this poſition, is, What is the common law of the land reſpecting the caſe in iſſue, *conſidered as a caſe of ſlavery?* It was ſaid, I remember, by one of the counſel, that the preſent ſtate of ſlavery among Negroes was totally different

from

from the ancient condition of villenage;
that it was a new fpecies of flavery utterly unknown to the common law of England. [*b*.]
In this opinion I readily coincide, and agree
with the learned gentleman. The next
queftion is, What do acts of parliament
fay on this head? I believe it muft be faid
for them, that they are, *enactively*, if I
may be allowed the expreffion, filent. If
this be fo, then the conclufion will operate

in

[*b*] It is faid in Mr. Hargrave's argument, p. 23.
" fuch was the expiring ftate of domeftic flavery in
Europe at the commencement of the 16th century,
when the difcovery of America and of the Weftern
and Eaftern coafts of Africa, gave occafion to the introduction of a new fpecies of flavery." If the arguer
had faid *a new fpecies of traffic*, inftead of a new fpecies of flavery, he had expreffed the real matter of
fact; feeing that the law by which this concern is
regulated, confiders it in no other light or view whatever. For this reafon too, it cannot be enumerated
among the feveral fpecies of flavery that he has mentioned, and taken notice of; each diftinct fpecies having its diftinct laws, appropriated thereto diftinctly,
as the laws of flavery. Among the Portuguefe and
Spaniards, I have been given to underftand, that Negroes are, and have ever been confidered, as with the
Englifh, matter of Property, and articles of commerce

D   in

in the nature of a plea to the jurifdiction of
your Lordfhip's Court. If the cafe be unknown to the common law, and acts of
parliament are filent thereupon, what bafis
muft your Lordfhip's judgment take?
Where there is no law, there can be no
remedy. If the common law be defective,
it is the bufinefs of acts of parliament to
fupply the defects : but until thofe defects
are fupplied, *fub judice lis eft*, and the matter

in the common courfe of traffic ; and were fo eftimated
by the French, until the refined age of Lewis XIV.
gave rife to a new inftitution of law, under the title
of the *Code noir*, for the particular government of
Negroes in their American colonies. It were to be
wifhed that a fit and proper digeft of this fort could
take place with us: but, I fear, the difficulty (which
arifes not fo much from the fubject, as from the means
of introduction) will prevent the execution of any
fuch plan. From the unlimited power of the Crown
of France, when laws are made, it is eafy to enforce an obedience to them : from the limited power
of our monarchy, fuch obedience is not to be exacted.
Each Englifh colony has a legiflature of its own ; and
although they all agree in the framing of laws not repugnant to the laws of England, yet they all widely
differ among themfelves in the mode and practice of
thofe laws.

muft

muſt remain undetermined. Your Lordſhip may however tell me, that, where
poſitive law is wanting, whereupon to
ground the deciſions of a Court, recourſe
may be had to the maxims and principles
of law, to the ſpirit of the conſtitution.
The reſult of this, my Lord, at beſt, is but
matter of opinion ; beſides, caſes founded
on the ſelf-ſame principles will often have
very different determinations, according
to the difference of circumſtances, and the
alteration or change of times. Thus, if it
had even been an original maxim of the
common law, that ſlavery was incompatible
with the frame and conſtitution of this
country, yet it does not therefore follow,
that occaſions have not ſince ariſen to com-
bat with this principle, and to juſtify particular concluſions differing from theſe general premiſes. For inſtance, my Lord,
the impreſſing of ſeamen, is an idea as
heterogeneous to the nature and eſſence of
this government, as ſlavery painted on the
blackeſt ground can be. It is ſlavery itſelf,

in

in its very definition; and what fignifies
the name, fays Hudibras, fince the thing
is the fame? But the indifpenfablenefs of
the meafure has neverthelefs (to continue
the metaphor) given colour to the practice,
and it is now feen in another light and
view. But to return: If your Lordfhip
fhould be of opinion, for opinion it muft
be, if there is no pofitive law to ground
your judgment upon, that Negroes in this
country are free, I will place in oppofition
to this, the opinions of the late Lord
Chancellour Hardwick, and his predeceffor
the Lord Chancellour Talbot, to wit, that
Negroes in this country are not free. Your
Lordfhip perceives, that I take your opinion upon fuppofition only; the other
opinions are well-known facts. To fearch
then for the grounds of your opinion,
without the certainty of its being fo,
would be now premature and unneceffary:
but, knowing the opinions of thefe two
great oracles of the law, it is of neceffity to
conclude, that they had the moft fufficient
foundation

foundation for them, feeing that it is allowed on every hand, that no opinion was ever given in any cafe whatever with greater folemnity, or more deliberation, than thefe were. Now, my Lord, to invefligate the reafons of thefe opinions, is one way, perhaps, to arrive at the truth: but to follow men like thefe, in their refearches, is a procedure fitted only to abilities fuch as your Lordfhip's are. As conjecture however is open to all, though pofitive knowledge is but the gift of a few; I fhall therefore venture to fuggeft what might in part have led the ideas of thefe great and wife men to the conclufion which they have drawn, namely, that Negroes in this country do not become free. I have before ftated, my Lord, and have agreed with one of the learned counfel, that the condition of flavery among Negroes is unknown to the common law of this land: that it is a new fpecies of flavery, which has arifen within, and not beyond, the memory of man, as is neceffary to the defcriptive qua-

2   lity

lity of this kind of law; and, therefore, being not under the comprehenfion, it cannot be within the abfolute provifion of it, however reduceable thereto it may be made, by analogy, implication, or conftruction. I have faid too, that acts of parliament are filent on this head. I have repeated what I had before ftated and faid, in order to draw this inference: that although the flavery of Negroes is unknown to the common law of this country, and acts of parliament are filent thereupon; yet *the right* which Mr. Steuart claims in the Negroe, Somerfet, is *a right* given him by act of parliament.

I muft then apprize your Lordfhip, that from this inftant it is my intention to drop the term Slavery, at leaft as a term in argument with me. It is an odious word, that engendered this law-fuit, and now feeds and fupports it with the fuel of heated paffions and imaginations. Inftead therefore of fuch prejudiced and unpopular ground, whereupon the cafe has hitherto

been

been made to stand, I shall take the liberty to remove its situation, to change its
point of view, and to rest it on the land
of *commercial Property*; from whence, perhaps, it will be seen, not only in a less of-
fensive light, but where also it may find a
foundation more solid and substantial for
its support.

It is matter of course, my Lord, to say,
that you are well acquainted with all the
acts of parliament relative to the royal
African company of England, from its
establishment by charter in the reign of
Charles the Second down to the present
time [c]. Now, my Lord, the end of this
company was trade : the object of that
trade

[c] I have referred to this period of the Negroe-
trade to Africa, because Acts of Parliament go no farther back in confirmation of it ; but its commencement was of much earlier date. It began in this country about the middle of the 15th century, and was
carried on by means of letters patent obtained by
individual traders for their private emolument, until
the growth of the English plantations in America, in
the next century, made it an object of such importance;

trade Negroes, as the preamble to the act
of the 23d of Geo. II. c. xxxi. thus exprefsly declares : " Whereas the trade to
" and from Africa is very advantageous to
" Great-Britain, and neceffary for fupply-
" ing the plantations and colonies there-
" unto belonging with a fufficient number
" of Negroes, at reafonable rates, it is
" therefore enacted, &c. &c." Whatever then, my Lord, is matter of trade,
your Lordfhip knows, muft be matter of

tance, as not only to render the eftablifhment of a company neceffary, but of fuch profit as to engage even
crowned heads to be concerned therein. The firft
charter was granted in the year 1661, in favour of the
Duke of York ; but being revoked by confent of par-
ties, it was renewed in the year 1663, with more ample
privileges than the former. The principal adventurers
here, were Queen Catharine of Portugal, Mary Queen
of France, the Duke of York, Henrietta Maria Duch-
efs of Orleans, Prince Rupert, and others of the Court.
Thus upon the ground of an exclufive Right was this
trade continued, till, by the vaft increafe of the colonies, it became, in the beginning of the prefent century, a weight too heavy for the fupport of prerogative ;
and fo falling under the protection of Parliament, was
made, as it now is, a free, open, and *national* concern.

property,

property. The idea of the one is necef-
farily involved in the other. But, my
Lord, thefe acts have not been content with
this general conftruction : they have gone
farther, and have themfelves fet the mark
and ftamp of property upon Negroes.
Whether, my Lord, the Legiflature is jufti-
fiable herein, or whether it has authority
by the laws of nature to do this, is not for
me to determine. It is, perhaps, a right,
like many other civil rights, eftablifhed
by power, and maintained by force: but
this is matter of fpeculation for the fpe-
culative. I here contend only, that the
fact is as I have ftated it to be; and as it
will appear by the ftatute of the 25th of
Geo. II. c. xl. " which was made for the
" application of a fum of money therein
" mentioned, granted to his Majefty, for
" making compenfation and fatisfaction to
" the Royal African company of England,
" for their charter, lands, forts, caftles,
" flaves, military ftores, and all other their
" effects whatfoever; and to *veft* the lands,
" forts, caftles, flaves, military ftores, and

E   " *all*

" *all other their effects,* in the company of
" merchants trading to Africa;" and
wherein it is enacted, that " the royal
" African company of England, from and
" after the tenth day of April one thousand
" seven hundred and fifty-two, shall be,
" and they are hereby, absolutely divested
" of and from their said charter, lands,
" forts, castles, and military stores, *canoe-*
" *men, castle-slaves,* and all *other their estate,*
" *property, and effects* whatsoever; and that
" all and every the British forts, lands,
" castles, settlements, and factories, on the
" coast of Africa, beginning at Port Sally,
" and extending from thence to the Cape of
" Good Hope inclusive, which were granted
" to the said company by the said charter,
" or which have been since erected or pur-
" chased by the said company; and all other
" the regions, countries, dominions, terri-
" tories, continents, coasts, ports, bays,
" rivers, and places, lying and being within
" the aforesaid limits, and the islands near
" adjoining to those coasts, and compre-
" hended within the limits described by
" the

" the faid charter; and which now are, or
" at any time heretofore have been, in the
" poffeffion of, or claimed by, the faid
" royal African company of England, to-
" gether with the cannon and other mili-
" tary ftores, *canoe-men, caftle-flaves*, at and
" belonging to the faid forts, caftles, fettle-
" ments, and factories, particularly men-
" tioned and fet forth in the firft fchedule
" to this act annexed (fuch ftores as have
" been made ufe of in the fervice of the
" forts, and fuch *canoe-men and flaves* as
" may have died fince the taking of the
" faid furvey, only excepted); and alfo all
" contracts and agreements made by or for,
" or on the behalf of, the faid royal African
" company, with any of the kings, princes,
" or natives, of any of the countries cr
" places on the faid coafts; and *all other*
" *the property, eftate, and effects* whatfoever,
" of the faid royal African company, fhall,
" from and after the faid tenth day of April
" one thoufand feven hundred and fifty-
" two, *be vefted in*, and the fame and every
" of them are and is hereby *fully and abfo-*
E 2 " *lutely*

" *lutely vefted in the faid corporation,* called
" and known by the name of ' The com-
" 'pany of merchants trading to Africa,' and
" their fucceffors, freed and abfolutely dif-
" charged of and from all claims and de-
" mands of the faid royal African company
" of England, and their creditors, and every
" of them, and of all and every perfon or
" perfons claiming under them, or any or
" either of them."

Here, my Lord, the *legal nature* of Negroes, if I may fo fpeak, is fully eftablifhed
and clearly afcertained, by act of parliament. Your Lordfhip perceives, that they
are *in hoc verbo* declared to be property, and
are vefted as goods and chattels, and as other
effects are, in owners prefcribed for them.
If it is obferved, my Lord, that the term
Slave is made ufe of, and recognized by
this act of parliament; it is anfwered, not
relatively fo, as to a ftate of flavery, but
defcriptively only of fuch things as fhall be
deemed the property and effects of this company. The ftatute, my Lord, of the 5th
of His prefent Majefty, ch. xliv. enacts,
" that

" that fuch parts of Africa as were ceded by the laft treaty of Paris, together with the goods, flaves, and other effects thereunto belonging, and which were, by a former act, vefted in the company of merchants trading to Africa, fhall now become the property of the Crown;" fo that the King, as well as this corporation of merchants, are, by the law of the land, poffeffed, and are now the actual and rightful owners, of a very confiderable number of Negroes, under the afore-mentioned defcription, of canoe-men, caftle-flaves, women, children, carpenters, and other artificers, particularly fet forth in fchedules annexed to the afore-mentioned acts. It is alfo enacted, " that the trade to Africa fhall be free and open to all His Majefty's fubjects, without preference or diftinction;" and it is further provided, " that thefe acts fhall be taken and deemed as public acts, and fhall be judicially taken notice of as fuch by all Judges, Juftices, and other perfons whatfoever, without fpecially pleading the

2   fame."

fame." Thus far, my Lord, do acts of parliament extend in the confirmation and establishment of this trade to Africa. I shall now beg leave to cite one statute more, in order unqueſtionably to prove what the ſenſe of the Legiſlature of this country is, with reſpect to the ſtate and condition of Negroes. This ſtatute, my Lord, is the 5th of Geo. II. c. viith, wherein (it being made for the more eaſy recovery of debts in His Majeſty's plantations and colonies in America (it is enacted "that,
" from and after the twenty-ninth day of
" September one thouſand ſeven hundred
" and thirty-two, the houſes, lands, *Ne-*
" *groes,* and other hereditaments and real
" eſtates, ſituate or being within any of the
" ſaid plantations, belonging to any perſon
" indebted, ſhall be liable to, and charge-
" able with, all juſt debts, duties, and de-
" mands, of what nature or kind ſoever,
" owing by any ſuch perſon to His Ma-
" jeſty, or any of his ſubjects, and ſhall
" and may be aſſets for the ſatisfaction
" thereof,

" thereof, in like manner as real eftates are
" by the law of England liable to the fa-
" tisfaction of debts due by bond or other
" fpecialty, and fhall be fubject to the like
" remedies, proceedings, and procefs, in
" any court of law or equity, in any of the
" faid plantations refpectively, for feizing,
" extending, felling, or difpofing, of any
" fuch houfes, lands, *Negroes*, and other
" hereditaments, and real eftates, towards
" the fatisfaction of fuch debts, duties, and
" demands, in like manner as perfonal
" eftates in any of the faid plantations re-
" fpectively are feized, extended, fold, or
" difpofed of, for the fatisfaction of fuch
" debts."

Herein then, my Lord, is not to be found even the trace of an idea of flavery confidered as fuch by Parliament, among Negroes : but, on the contrary, what their legal ftate and condition is, is conceived and expreffed in terms fo plain and clear, fo explicit and precife, that the moft fceptical cannot doubt the meaning, nor the moft fimple fail to underftand it. They

are,

are, as houfes, lands, hereditaments, and real eftate, affets; and, in like manner as perfonal eftate, to be difpofed of, for the payment of debts due to the King and his fubjects.

Upon this ftate and expofition then, my Lord, of thefe feveral ftatutes, it would feem that I am well warranted, by their authority, in my idea, that the right which Mr. Steuart claims in the Negroe Somerfet, is a right given him by act of parliament; and confirmed in my propofition, that this is a cafe of property.

But, my Lord, in order fully to eftablifh this doctrine, it may perhaps be expected, that I fhould not only fhew what the law is, but that I fhould prove alfo what the law is not; and this muft necef-farily lead me to reafon fomewhat more clofely on the fubject.

I am aware it may be objected, my Lord, that property in Negroes fo vefted, is a property created in Africa for the ufe and purpofe of the colonies in America: from

whence

whence a queftion will be deduced, Whether Negroes are property in England?

It appears, my Lord, that a trade is opened, with the fanction, and now under the protection of parliament, between the fubjects of Great Britain and the natives or inhabitants of Africa. The medium of this trade on the one hand are, manufactures, goods, wares, and other merchandize: on the other, captive Negroes, or flaves; which, for thefe commodities, are given in barter and exchange. It will be allowed, I prefume, my Lord, that thefe Britifh traders, or merchants, have an abfolute property in their merchandize; to truck and to traffic with this merchandize is the legal inftitution of the trade: it will be abfurd then to deny, that they have not an equal intereft in the thing received, as they had in the thing given. To avoid this dilemma then, the objection recurs; that, in Africa they may have an intereft, in America they may have the fame, in Europe they have none: but affertion without proof, is argument without weight. Where

F   is

is the law that has drawn this line of diftinction? Is there any act of parliament,
or claufe of an act of parliament, that has
fixed and defcribed the zones or climates
wherein property in Negroes may be held,
or where it may not be held? Until I am
better informed, my Lord, I muft take for
granted, that no fuch law exifts; and if
no fuch law does exift, the manifeft conclufion is, that where property is once legally vefted, it muft legally remain; until
altered or extinguifhed by fome power co-
equal to that which gave it [d].

But

[d] Mr. Hargrave fays, in his argument, p. 67.
" Another objection will be, that there are Englifh acts
of parliament, which give a fanction to the flavery of
Negroes; and therefore that it is now lawful, whatever it might be antecedently to thofe ftatutes. The
ftatutes in favour of this objection are the 5th of
Geo. II. ch. 7, which makes Negroes in America
liable to all debts, fimple contract as well as fpeciality,
and the ftatutes regulating the African trade, particularly the 23d Geo. II. ch. 31, which in the preamble
recites that the trade to Africa is advantageous to Great
Britain, and neceffary for fupplying its colonies with
Negroes. But the utmoft which can be faid of thefe
ftatutes

But as it may perhaps be to the purpofe, my Lord, to try the force and effect
of thefe acts of trade referred to, I will,
with your Lordfhip's indulgence, ftate a
cafe or two, whereby their operation in this
country might be felt and perceived.

Suppofe, my Lord, that a fleet of mer-
chant fhips belonging to the African company, containing twenty thoufand Negroes
on board (more or lefs, it is of no matter),
bound from Africa to America, fhould, by
ftrange,

ftatutes is, that they impliedly authorize the flavery of
Negroes in America ; and it would be a ftrange thing
to fay, that permitting flavery there, includes a per-
miffion of flavery here. By an unhappy concurrence of
circumftances, the flavery of Negroes is thought to have
become neceffary in America ; and therefore in America our Legiflature has permitted the flavery of Negroes.
But the flavery of Negroes is unneceffary in England,
and therefore the Legiflature has not extended the per-
miffion of it to England ; and not having done fo, how
can this Court be warranted to make fuch an exten-
fion ?" Now this is the very affertion without proof that
I have complained of above, and have there fully anfwered : but, in truth, the beft anfwer it can receive, is
its own futility. Why did not Mr. Hargrave, inftead
of his *ipfe dixit*, produce authorities to fet afide this

objection?

ſtrange, contrary, and adverſe winds, be driven and wrecked upon the coaſt of England; that the ſhips were loſt and deſtroyed, but that the Negroes had been landed in ſafety on this ſhore of freedom : would the African company, my Lord, be juſtified and entitled to re-ſhip theſe Negroes in other veſſels, to the end that they might be conveyed to their deſtined ports in America? Or, would the pure air of this country, as has been inſiſted on, ſet them, with caps of liberty on their heads, free and at

objection? He is on other occaſions not ſparing of proofs and citations. But what is his *ipſe dixit?* It is this :

The Legiſlature has permitted the ſlavery of Negroes in America :

But the ſlavery of Negroes is unneceſſary in England :

Ergo, the Legiſlature has not extended the permiſſion of it to England.

This is his mode of reaſoning, and theſe are his very words, which, when examined ſyllogiſtically, ſhew, if I have not forgotten my logic, that they are as little conformable to rule, as to matter of fact. But, the fact is, Mr. Hargrave has found this objection a ſtumbling block in his way, and therefore, nimbly leaping over it himſelf, has left it to trip up the heels of his followers.

large;

large; thereby robbing, for so I muſt call it, theſe merchants of their property to the amount of one million of money, at the allowance, and on the moderate computation, of fifty pounds price for each individual Negroe? In this kingdom of commerce, my Lord, where the rights of merchants are ſo well diſtinguiſhed, and the laws of trade are ſo minutely known, I ſhould preſume that the caſe would not admit of a queſtion. Of what uſe would the charter of this company be to them, if the laws protective of that charter ſhould be found inadequate and ineffectual to the maintenance and ſecurity of their property? But again : it has been obſerved, that by the ſtatute of the 5th of George III. chap. xliv. a number of canoe-men, and other Negroes, in Africa, were veſted in the Crown. Now, by canoe-men, I ſuppoſe, my Lord, are meant, African ſailors. Suppoſe then, that one hundred, for example, of theſe ſailors ſhould, by

2   ſome

some contrivance or other, find their way into England; would the King, my Lord, have authority to remand them to their place of duty? or, would writs of Habeas Corpus, in despite of this act of Parliament, protect them here; thereby determining the right of the Crown in them? The case, my Lord, speaks and determines for itself. Wherein then, my Lord, differs the case of Mr. Steuart from these? Their importance is greater, but the principle throughout is the same. I believe it is not denied that Mr. Steuart was the *bona fide* purchaser of Somerset, in the legal course of trade. I do not apprehend that any evidence was offered to shew that he had stolen him, or that he came by him otherwise surreptitiously. If my memory does not fail me, the property was proved, by affidavit, before your Lordship; or it was stated in the return made to the Writ of Habeas Corpus; but in either way it is of no concern, since the title-deeds are

not

not now before the Court as the objects of
of Litigation [*e*].

[*e*] With refpect to the ftatute of the 5th of Geo. II.
c. 7. there are not wanting frequent inftances of its
having been inforced in this country ; particularly in a
cafe of the noted Rice : who, forging a Letter of Attorney with intent to defraud the Bank of England of a
confiderable fum of money, fled to France, was delivered up by that Court, and afterwards hanged at Tyburn.
It feems, upon his abfconding, a commiffion of Bank-
ruptcy was awarded againft him ; and the Commiffion-
ers, as I am credibly informed, under this very Act of
Parliament here mentioned, fold a Negroe of his in the
city of London, as his property, and among his other
goods and chattels, for the fatisfaction of the creditors.
But this act does not require cafes for its confirmation,
neither is it the place where executed that I contend
for ; it is *the vefting of the property*, without provifo or
condition, that furmounts all objection.   Suppofe I had
purchafed a Negroe in the ifland of Barbadoes, or in any
other part of America, that had been extended there at
the fuit of the King for a debt due to him, and had
brought this Negroe with me to England : would Mr.
Hargrave, or any other lawyer, fay, that a writ of Habeas Corpus, or any other writ whatfoever *not founded on
the verdict of a jury*, could difpoffefs me of a property,
which I held under the fenfe, letter, and fpirit of an Act
of Parliament ? Can any implication of law operate
againft the exprefs words and meaning of a law ? And
would not fuch argument in its confequences be a mere
reductio ad abfurdum ?

Here

Here then, my Lord, without farther difquifition, I might venture to reft the defence of Mr. Steuart, and therein the law of the cafe itfelf. The reafoning, perhaps, may be faid to be new, and it is opinion only of my own that fupports the doctrine : but, I truft, that, upon examination, it will be found to be not therefore the lefs conclufive. However, as I am upon the fubject, it may not be amifs that I fhould purfue it fomewhat farther; and, by extending the chain of enquiry, ftrengthen and enforce the arguments that have been already offered and applied. It was faid, by one of the plaintiff's counfel, that municipal laws were binding only in the ftate wherein they were made; that, as foon as a member of that ftate was out of it, they ceafed to have their influence on him; and the laws of nature of courfe fucceeded to him. As a general propofition, my Lord, this might have had its admiffion; but even as fuch, it is not without its exception. I think I have the moft

classical

claffical authority of the law to fay otherwife. For inftance, allegiance, which is
the duty that every fubject owes to the
fovereign, or fovereignty, of that particular
ftate to which he belongs, is a municipal
law; and yet, neither time, place, nor cir-
cumftance, can alter, forfeit, or cancel, the
obligation. An Englifhman (fays Judge
Blackftone) [f], who removes to France
or to China, owes the fame allegiance to
the King of England there as at home,
and twenty years hence as well as now.
But, my Lord, with regard to the particular application of this propofition, when
the gentleman endeavoured to make a diftinction between the laws of the colonies
and the laws of England, in my apprehenfion he was extremely miftaken. I fancy
the relationfhip and dependency of the
children colonies on their mother country
did not occur to his mind. The circum-
ftance of their having internal laws of their
own, by no means argues a difference in

[f] Vide Blackftone's Commentaries, vol. i. p. 369.

G   thofe

thofe laws, independent of the laws of England. As well might it be faid, that the laws of England are not the laws of the county of Kent, becaufe by the cuftom of gavelkind they differ from the general laws in the difpofition of Eftates; and fo of Borough-Englifh, and wherever in this kingdom particular cuftoms are to be found or met with. For, my Lord, it is not only a firft and leading principle of legiflation in the colonies, arifing out of their original grants and charters, and enforced by the royal inftructions given to commanders in chief there; but it is alfo enacted by the ftatute of the 7th and 8th of William III. ch. xxii. " that no law, ufage, or cuftom, fhall be made or received in the plantations, repugnant to the laws of England:" fo that, by thefe reftrictions, the very *leges loci* (wherein, from fituation, from climate, and from other circumftances, one might naturally fuppofe fome difference) are forced as much as may be to a conformity with the conftitution and laws of this country;

and to prevent even the accident of a contrary occurrence, your Lordſhip knows, that there is a counſellour appointed to the board of trade here, whoſe eſpecial buſineſs it is, to examine all the colony acts, and thereupon to make his report, if neceſſary, previous to the royal confirmation of them. If property, therefore, in Negroes, was repugnant to the law of England, it could not be the law of America : for (beſides the reaſons already aſſigned) by the ſame ſtatute wherever this repugnancy is, there the law is *ipſo facto* null and void. But I will further endeavour to elucidate this matter, by begging a queſtion or two, by way of caſe in point. Let it be admitted then, that a colony of Engliſh had embarked from hence, in order to eſtabliſh ſettlements for themſelves in ſome one of the late ceded iſlands in the Weſt Indies, and that they were arrived, it may be ſaid, in the iſland, *where Engliſh troops, trampling on the laws of God and man, are ſlaughtering even to extirpation a guiltleſs*

race

race of Caribs, the aborigines of the country.
I mean the island of St. Vincent, an island
under the tutelage of a Saint too! And
suppose that, upon their arrival there, the
Legiflature of that country had taken it
into their heads to pafs an act fimilar to the
25th of Geo. II. ch. xl. already referred to,
thereby vefting thefe people as property, in
certain owners allotted to them : I fhould
be glad to know, my Lord, whether this
act could poffibly have operated as a law,
and whether it was not, *eo inflanti*, upon
its being enacted, deflitute and void of all
force, validity, and effect ? Your Lordfhip's anfwer doubtlefs would be, that this
act muft have been its own executioner,
that it was *felo de fe*. Why then, my
Lord, does not the principle directive of
this conclufion on the cafe of the colony of
Englifh, determine likewife on the cafe of
the Negroes ? If an act of an American
plantation making property of a colony of
Englifh there, is nullified *ab initio* from its
being

being enacted, why is not an act making property of a colony of Africans fufceptible of the fame nullity? The reafon, my Lord, is twofold : firft, becaufe in the one act, fuch a law is not only repugnant to, but abfolutely fubverfive of, the laws of England : fecondly, becaufe in the other act, fuch a law is not only confiftent with, but founded on, the laws of England : and this, my Lord, proves to mathematical demonftration, that the colony laws are not only in general dependant on the laws of England, but, in particular inftances, owe their origin and fource to them : fo that, as the refracted rays of light, diverging from one point through a prifm, may be concentred in the fame focus ; in like manner may thefe laws, notwithftanding their number and variety, be collected and difpofed of in one common fyftem or digeft, as parts of the fame whole. From what therefore I have here fuggefted, my Lord, I mean to conclude generally, that the right and property, not only of Mr. Steuart in his

Negroe

Negroe Somerset, but of every subject of
Great Britain in his Negroe or Negroes,
either in the colonies or elsewhere, is a
right and property founded in him by the
law of this land; that the royal grants,
letters patent, and charters, for and of the
African trade and company, confirmed and
established by acts of Parliament, are the
foundation whereupon all the laws of the
colonies, respecting their Negroes, are
built; and that, without such sanction,
those laws could never have been made.
For, my Lord, it is evident that the colonies could not have had power of themselves to institute this trade to Africa; neither have they the means to support it.
Without this trade then to Africa, no Negroes could have been imported to them;
and if they had had no Negroes among
them, they had needed no laws appertain-
ing to Negroes [g].

But

[g] Mr. Hargrave further says, in his argument, p.
67 and 68, " The slavery of Negroes being admitted
to be lawful *now* in America, however questionable its
first introduction there might be, it may be urged that
the

But, my Lord, it may· be urged, that
although the laws of England may make
property of Negroes, they do not make
flaves of them. I fhould imagine that, although an individual, I might anfwer in-
dividually for every American fubject of

the *lex loci* ought to prevail, and that the mafter's property in the Negroe as a flave having had a lawful commencement in America, cannot be juftly varied by
bringing him into England." This is one among other
objections raifed by Mr. Hargrave in order to receive
his anfwer. Now as to the doubt exprefled here, namely, " however queftionable its firft introduction there
might be," the right of granting letters patent, and of
erecting corporations for the purpofes of trade, being
the undoubted prerogative of the king as arbiter of the
commerce of his dominions; the lawfulnefs of this trade
to Africa is no more to be queftioned whilft it was
carried on under this direction, than it is to be queftioned now it is under the controul of parliament. It was
before conftitutionally legal, it is now parliamentary
fo : but the anfwer to the objection itfelf is as little fa-
tisfactory as the doubt is. Here a moft unnatural diftinction is aimed at between the colony laws in America, and the laws of their mother country : putting the
lex loci of thefe colonies upon the fame footing with
the *lex loci* of Ruffia or Pruffia, or any other foreign
country : whereas the *lex loci* of the colonies is founded
on the *lex loci* of England, and is, *in totidem verbis*, the
fame, as has been made to appear.

the

the King, that they do not defire any greater intereft in their Negroes than that of property. It is felf-fufficient to anfwer all their purpofes, and to produce all that great good which this nation experiences therefrom. It is a fuppofition of inhumanity, I hope, inapplicable to thefe people, that they fhould wifh to make flaves of their Negroes, merely for the fake of flavery ; and if it fhould appear, that there is no fuch law exifting in America, as the law of flavery, confidered as fuch, I fhould infer that the contrary prefumption was fitteft to be entertained and received. The law refpecting Negroes there, my Lord, is the law of property, confentaneous to the law of England. By this law they are made real eftate, for the purpofe of defcent, and goods and chattels *quoad* the payment of debts. This is the original and fundamental law concerning Negroes. I do not remember ever to have feen the word Slavery made ufe of, in any law, of any colony, in America. I admit that Ne-

groes

groes are there termed flaves : but I will tell your Lordfhip why. In the criminal law, where they become neceffarily the objects of punifhment, it is effential that they fhould have fome defcriptive name or title given to them. It is for this rea-fon, therefore, that they are there, and there only fo called. As they had been already defined to be property, as Negroes, it could not be faid that, if property fhould ftrike his mafter, property fhall be punifh-ed; but it is faid, that if a flave fhould ftrike his mafter, this flave fhall be punifh-ed accordingly. Now in the antient law of England, my Lord, when flavery was part of the conftitution, your Lordfhip knows, that not only the villein was de-fcribed, but the law of villenage or bond-age was alfo known and laid down. In the laws of America, the flave is made mention of, for the reafon affigned ; but the law of flavery, however impliedly, is no where exprefsly to be found.

H   But

But here, my Lord, I muſt beg leave to make a ſhort digreſſion, intentionally to wipe off an imputation, which by one of the plaintiff's counſel was thrown on the owners and poſſeſſors of Negroes in America. In the courſe of his pleading, he took occaſion to draw a horrid and a frightful picture of the barbarity, and cruelties, that were exerciſed on theſe beings in the colonies ; and concluded with hoping, that ſuch practices would for ever remain forbidden to this country. Your Lordſhip knows, that wherever order is, there diſcipline muſt enſue. Like as cauſe and effect, they are inſeparable one from the other. Now it is not to be preſumed, that an hundred thouſand Negroes are to be held in obedience to ten or fifteen thouſand owners (for this perhaps may be found to be near the average) without ſome means or methods, which, from their accidental application, might ſo generally operate on their fears, as to produce the end required. It is ſo in the caſe of the

navy ;

navy; it is fo in the army of every country in the known world. A foldier would
not put himfelf in the front of a battle, to
run the rifque of being fhot through the
head, if he did not know that this would
be the certain confequence of his defer-
tion. The fear of the latter gives him
courage to engage in the former : or, how
otherwife could fifty officers, perhaps,
command a regiment of a thoufand men?
But, my Lord, the defign of this gentleman's groupe of figures, was to induce a
belief in the Court, that Englifh feelings
were to revolt at American punifhments.
As martial law is not the law of Weftmin-
fter-hall, it is likely that he has not ftudied
it : but, living in this country, I cannot
fuppofe him a ftranger to the effects of it.
Who have not been eye-witneffes to the
hundreds of ftripes that have been given to
foldiers on the parade of St. James's ? I
faw once, my Lord, two failors [who were
perhaps impreffed men too] under the
fentence of receiving five hundred lafhes
H 2 each,

each, flogged on their naked backs along the sides of thirty-four men of war, lying at anchor in the harbour of Spithead. Was such a punishment ever known to have been inflicted on any Negroe in the American plantations? No, my Lord: the laws of every colony forbid it: but a stronger law than these prevents it, the law of self-interest. Negroes are the riches of those who possess them. Land, without their aid and assistance, in order to cultivation, is useless, and of no value. If their healths are impaired, their labour is lost, and profit ceases. If their lives are destroyed, their places must be supplied with more difficulty, and at a much greater expence, than is commonly supposed. The good consequence of which, my Lord, is, that the state of Negroes, *cæteris paribus*, in America, is preferable, nay infinitely more desireable, than the condition of the poorer sort of people residing even in this boasted happy isle. I will not say, my Lord, that this is a rule without an exception. There are madmen

in

in all parts of the world, who, as such, act diametrically oppofite to their intereft. Such there are in America : but your Lordfhip fees, that the obfervation is founded on reafon ; and I can affure your Lordfhip, that it is the effect of general experience. But, my Lord, I cannot quit this fubject without making all due allowance for the learned counfel's zeal for his client, and for the warmth of his youth, which probably might have hurried him into this ill-grounded and uncalled-for reproach. It was ill-grounded, as, I hope, I have proved : it was uncalled-for, becaufe not neceffary to the queftion; and could no otherwife have been applied or received, than as mere *argumenta ad paffiones:* which, however admiffable to the ears of a jury, to the diftinguifhing eye of a court, never fail to carry with them their own impropriety. But in juftice to the gentleman, in other refpects, I am called upon to fay, that it was with infinite pleafure I perceived thofe rays of genius and abilities in him, which

2   promife

promife to fhine forth fo confpicuoufly, to the ornament of this country, and to the honour of Barbadoes, his native ifland, in America *.　　-

I come now, my Lord, to fay, that I hope it will not be imputed to me as vanity, that I have ventured to fuggeft what might in part have led the ideas of thofe great and wife men, the Lord Chancellours Talbot and Hardwick, to the conclufion which they have drawn, namely, that Negroes in this country do not become free. I was encouraged in the undertaking, by the greatnefs of their authority. I was enlightened in the purfuit, by the evidence of their opinion. I thought myfelf juftified in refting their chief reafons and motives on the principles of property; and I will produce the opinion itfelf, as the warrant of my juftification :

" We are of opinion, That a flave, by
" coming from the Weft Indies, either
" with or without his mafter, to Great-
" Britain or Ireland, doth not become

* This was a Mr. Alleyne.

" free;

" free ; and that his mafter's *property* or
" *right* in him is not thereby determined
" or varied ; and baptifm doth not beftow
" freedom on him, nor make any altera-
" tion in his temporal condition in thefe
" kingdoms : We are alfo of opinion, that
" the mafter may *legally* compel him to
" return to the plantations [*b*].

Jan. 24, 1729.   " P. YORK.
                      " C. TALBOT."

Upon this opinion, my Lord, I fhall
make no other remark, than that right and
property feem to be the obvious ground and
foundation of it, or the hinges whereupon
the whole is made to hang and to turn.

But, my Lord, I will now admit, that,
what is held to be law, is at variance with
this opinion. It is laid down " that a
" Slave or Negroe, the inftant he lands in

[*b*] This opinion was repeated by Lord Hardwick,
fitting as Chancellour, twenty years after it had been
given, with additional affurances, and under the fulleft
conviction of its ftrict conformity to the law.

                       " England,

" England, becomes a freeman;" that is,
" the law will protect him in the enjoy-
" ment of his perfon and his property;
" yet with regard to any right which the
" mafter may have acquired to the perpe-
" tual fervice of John or Thomas, this will
" remain exactly in the fame ftate as be-
" fore." The interpreters of this law, my
Lord, may be *right* in point of *reafon*;
but, I fubmit it, that they are *wrong* in
point of *law* [*i*]. The cafe is this, my Lord:
feeing that Negroes are human creatures,
it would feemingly follow that they fhould
be allowed the privileges of their nature,
which, in this country particularly, are in
part the enjoyment of perfon and property. Now, from hence a relation is in-
ferred, that has not the leaft colour of
exiftence in law. A Negroe is looked upon

[*i*] It is faid, *Lex eft fumma ratio.* I am forry that
fo excellent a rule of law fhould admit of contra-
diction; and I wifh that this was the only inftance of
an exception: but, let it be confidered, whether our
Game laws, our Marriage acts, and, for the moft part,
the penal laws of this country, *cum multis aliis quæ, &c.*
are not contrary both to reafon and nature.

to

to be the fervant of his mafter; but by what authority is the relation of *fervant* and *mafter* created? Not by the authority of the law, however it may be by the evidence of reafon. By the law, the relation is, as *Negroe* and *Owner:* he is made matter of trade; he is an article of commerce, he is faid to be property; he is goods, chattels, and effects, veftable and vefted in his owner. This, my Lord, is the law of England, however contradictory to, or fubverfive of, the law of reafon [*k*].

Now as to the fact of property in Negroes, without exception to this kingdom or limitation to other countries, I am fupported in opinion by the authority of the learned Judge Blackftone; though he afcribes the rife of this property to a fource very different from me. In the chapter of, Title to

[*k*] " It is laid down," fays Judge Blackftone, that
" acts of parliament contrary to reafon are void: but
" if the parliament will pofitively enact a thing to be
" done which is *unreafonable*, I know of no power that
" can controul it."——V. his Comm, Vol. I. p. 91.

I   things

things perfonal by occupancy, he fays,
" As in the goods of the enemy, fo alfo
" in his perfon, a man may acquire a fort
" of qualified property, by taking him a
" prifoner in war, at leaft till his ranfom
" be paid. And this doctrine feems to have
" been extended to Negroe fervants, who
" are purchafed when captives, of the na-
" tions with whom they are at war, and
" continue therefore in fome degree the
" *property of their mafters* (he fhould have
" rather faid *owners)* who buy them." Here
then he refers to the law of nations, for
the eftablifhment of that which I appeal
to the law of England for. Now, although
the law of nations might have been a good
ground to reft the municipal law of this
country upon, and might have ferved as a
preamble to, or reafon for, an act of parliament; yet it is not within my conception,
how, in fuch an internal concern as this is,
the law of nations could have been the law
itfelf. For example, if in the return to
the writ of Habeas Corpus in this cafe, it
had been fet forth, that Negroe fervants are
pur-

purchafed when captives of the nations with whom they are at war, and therefore the *law of nations* gives their mafters a property in their perfons ; would your Lordfhip have thought this a *lawful* plea for the remanding of Somerfet ? If not, your Lordfhip finds that the fact of property is admitted by the learned Judge, without the proper foundation of law to fupport it. But he proceeds to fay, " though, *accurately fpeaking,* that property confifts rather in the perpetual fervice, than in the body or perfon of the captives." *Accurately fpeaking,* my Lord, I join iffue with the learned Judge: but, *legally fpeaking,* the law is as he had ftated it to be. Thofe who fpeak accurately reafon from the real nature of Negroes, and draw their conclufions from thence : the Lords Talbot and Hardwick fpoke legally, and drew their opinions from the fountain-head of law. Befides, my Lord, I conceive it to be impoffible that the law fhould be as thefe interpreters or reporters have made it to be ; becaufe the refult of it is plain-

incon-

inconfiftency, and pofitive abfurdity. If
Somerfet is protected by the law of England in the enjoyment of his perfon and
property, how, in appeal to common fenfe,
can Mr. Steuart's right in him remain
exactly in the fame ftate as before? " Yes,
it may be faid, he has a right to the perpetual fervice of him; for this is no more
than the fame ftate of fubjection for life,
which every apprentice fubmits to for the
fpace of feven years, or fometimes for a
longer time." But by what mode or me-
thod does Mr. Steuart acquire this perpetual right to his fervice? There is no in-
denture of apprenticefhip on the part of
Somerfet to him : there is no written contract of any fort or kind whatever, there is
no parole agreement between them, to enforce this right of fervice. How is it to
be maintained then? If by the purchafe of
him, property is the offspring of purchafe;
and, as fuch, Mr. Steuart claims him. If
he is not his property, he has otherwife no
right in him, nor to his fervices; and,
again, if he is his property, who fhall dif-
feife him thereof?

As

As I began, my Lord, with making a diftinction between flavery and property, and have perfifted in their legal difference relatively to the ftate and condition of Negroes, fome farther explanation on this point may perhaps be looked for and required of me. I am fenfible it may objectively be faid, that in every kind of flavery there is an included degree of property, more or lefs limited or extended; and that this kind of property therefore in Negroes is but an accumulated degree of flavery: fo that the diftinction I have made is a diftinction without a difference, and a mere contentioufnefs about words. But, although I admit the truth of this objection in part, I muft deny, in the whole, its application to the principles of my argument. Slavery, my Lord, is that ftate of fubjection, which mankind, by force or otherwife, acquire *the one over the other.* In every fociety therefore where this ftate of fubjection prevails, the object and fubject of thofe laws neceffary for the regulation thereof are, what? *are human nature itfelf.*

I   Let

Let it be confidered then whether *human nature* is either the object or fubject of the laws of England, refpecting the ftate and condition of Negroes. And here, my Lord, I beg leave to affert, that the appeal I have already made to thofe laws maintains the contrary matter of fact, with the unde‐ niable proof of felf-evidence. But it may again be urged, that authority, however refpectable, is not the teft of truth; and therefore, fays the difputant, fhew me the reafon, the *Cur*, the *Quare*, the *Quamob‐ rem*, of thefe laws. To which, in the lan‐ guage and poftulate of the Greek Philofo‐ pher, I reply; that, as matter of fact is the Δὸς πᾶ ςῶ of my argument, beyond this, it is not incumbent on me to extend my enquiries. And yet, my Lord, a refearch of this nature being perhaps founded upon no impertinent or unmeaning curiofity, the fuggeftions even of fancy and imagination may not be here undeferving your Lord‐ fhip's attention; and as fuch the fubject is, in this view, of courfe not unworthy my notice. It being then evidently the will,

it

it is not to be prefumed, till the contrary
appears, that it was the effect alfo of the
wifdom of parliament, that Negroes under the law fhould not be confidered as
human beings; and therefore I am led to
furmife that this determination of the Legiflature might have arifen from one or
the other of two motives or confiderations:
the one *phyfical*, the other *political*. With
refpect then to the phyfical motive, your
Lordfhip need not be told how much the
origin of Negroes, the caufe of that re-
markable difference in complexion from
the reft of mankind, and the woolly covering of their heads fo fimilar to the fleece
of fheep, have puzzled and perplexed the
Naturalifts of all countries for ages paft.
It was a fubject of the deepeft reflection to
the great and learned Mr. Boyle; and what
could engage his divine abilities, without
fatisfaction either to himfelf or others,
is likely to remain among thofe *arcana* of
nature that are not to be revealed to human
underftanding. But, although thefe phæ-
nomena in nature are not to be accounted

for,

for, and therefore admit of no principle of law inferible from them; yet their very incomprehenfiblenefs, when compared with other circumftances more known and better underftood, may ferve to this end, as fo many leffer weights in the fcales of greater probability. Now, my Lord, it is an opinion *univerfally* received, that human nature is *univerfally* the fame: but I fhould apprehend that this was a propofition rather taken for granted, than admitted to be proved: for although the proper ftudy of mankind is man, and therefore the univerfality of fuch an opinion is *prima facie* evidence of its truth; yet, it is to be obferved, that, of all other ftudies, the fcience of man has been leaft of all cultivated and improved. Man only, who examines all Nature elfe, ftands unexamined by himfelf. If we look into the vegetable and mineral kingdoms of this world, we fhall perceive a fcrutiny made in them the moft nice, accurate, and comprehenfive; we fhall find thefe grand divifions of nature

arranged

arranged in claffes, orders, kinds, and
forts : we fhall contemplate fyftems mo-
rally perfect. If we take a view of the
animal kingdom below ourfelves, we fhall
be witneffes there alfo of the fame order,
regularity, and perfection. Why then is
human nature exempt from this difquifition and arrangement ? Are men afraid to
turn their eyes upon themfelves, left they
behold themfelves in the mirror of truth ?
Or is it pride, or vanity, that caufes this
neglect? Yes, men would be angels, angels
would be gods, fays Mr. Pope [*l*] ; and
yet man, as Dr. Lifter obferves [*m*], is as
very a quadruped as any animal on earth ;
and whofe actions are moft of them refolva-
ble into inftinct, notwithftanding the principles which cuftom and education have
fuperinduced. Of other animals then, it
is well known, there are many *kinds*, each
kind having its proper *fpecies* fubordinate
thereto : but man is one kind of animal,
and yet, without diftinction of fpecies,

[*l*] Vid. his Effay on Man.
[*m*] Vid. his Journ. to Paris.

K   *univerfally,*

univerfally the fame. Does not this feem to break in upon and unlink that great chain of Heaven, which in due gradation joins and unites the whole with all its parts? May it not be mcre perfective of the fyftem to fay, that human nature is a *clafs*, comprehending an *order* of beings, of which man is the *genus*, divided into diftinct and feparate *fpecies* of men? All other fpecies of the animal kingdom have their marks of diftinction: why fhould man be univerfally indifcriminate one to the other?

The great Mr. Locke fays [*n*], that reafon is fuppofed to make the characteriftic difference between man and beafts: but, what is the characterftic that diftinguifhes man from man? That there may and fhould be fuch a diftinction, I have already endeavoured to fhew; and I am apt to think that this is a queftion not without its anfwer. The learned Dr. Hutchinfon [*o*] has demonftrated the exiftence of *a moral fenfe* in, and peculiar to, human nature;

[*n*] Vid. his Effay on Human Underftanding.
[*o*] Vid. his Moral Philofophy.

which

which as it ferves effentially to diftinguifh
man from beafts, and to raife him from
the tenth to the ten thoufandth link of the
chain, fo is it, in my humble apprehenfion,
an evident criterion of the fpecific difference between man and man. Now Mr.
Locke, fpeaking of reafon as that faculty
whereby man is diftinguifhed from beafts,
fays, that beafts have reafon in common
with men ; in which however he is to be
underftood, that beafts poffefs the faculty,
and in fome meafure have the ufe, of reafon;
but man's fuperiority over beafts confifts in
the power of exerting that faculty, and in
the compound ratio of its exertion. As
beafts therefore have the faculty of reafon,
and it is the exertion in degree of that
faculty (particularly in obtaining abftraƈt
ideas) that creates the great difference between man and beafts : fo by the fame
parity of reafoning, the *moral fenfe* being a
faculty of the human mind common to all
men, the capacity of perceiving moral relations, the power of exercifing that facul-

ty,

ty, and the compound ratio of its exercife,
is that which makes the grand difference
and diftinction between man and man.
All nature, my Lord, which is the art of
God, is wifely fitted and adapted to that ufe
and purpofe for which it was ordained;
and the fame obfervation is to be made even
in the art of man. A flea is not lefs perfect than an elephant becaufe of its fize:
neither is the cup that holds a pint lefs
compleat than the veffel that contains an
hundred gallons; when both are full, the
end for which both were defigned is anfwered and fulfilled. The ufe then to be
made of this doctrine, my Lord, is, that
as experience, obfervation, and experiment,
are the foundations upon which all fpecu-
lative philofophy is raifed; fo, from experience and obfervation, I judge that the
truth of this hypothefis may be very clearly
proved and demonftrated. Now, in order
to this, it is neceffary to have recourfe to
the hiftories of nations: to read, to examine, and compare them, one with the
other. To obferve the moral improvements

2   had

had by them, to remark the focial virtues
that prevail; and this will bring me to the
accounts that have been given of Negroes
(for hiftories they have none of their own)
and confequently back to the fubject of this
addrefs to your Lordfhip. But, my Lord,
forbearing to trouble your Lordfhip with a
detail of thefe accounts, I fhall, referring
them to your Lordfhip's memory, content
myfelf with the bare mention of a few
facts only [*p*].

Mr.

[*p*] In looking into Mr. Hume's Effays, particularly
the one of *national characters* (which I had never feen
till after the above argument was finifhed) I was made
happy to obferve the ideas of fo ingenious a writer cor-
refponding with my own : but as we differ in fome refpects, and much of what I have fuggefted has been not
at all taken notice of by him, I fhall beg leave to infert
here what he has faid upon the fubject. " There is,"
fays he, " fome reafon to think, that all nations, which
live beyond the polar circles, or betwixt the tropics,
are inferior to the reft of the fpecies, and are *utterly incapable* of all the higher attainments of the human mind."
Upon which he has the following note : " I am apt to
fufpect the Negroes, and in general all the other *fpecies*
of men (for there are four or five different *kinds*) to be
naturally inferior to the whites." Now I do not apprehend, that, in order to have different *fpecies* of men, it is

at

Mr. Guthrie, in his account of Africa from the tropic of Cancer to the Cape of Good Hope, fays, " The hiftory of this continent is little known, and probably affords

at all neceffary to have four or five different *kinds*. I infer, that there is but *one genus* or *kind* of man (under the term *mankind*) fubordinate to which there are feveral *forts* or *fpecies* of men, differing from each other upon the principle that I have affigned ; and, as Hudibras fays,

> If one will do,
> What need of two ?

Befides, it is feemingly a lefs fyftematical arrangement. But he proceeds to fay, " There never was a civilized nation of any other complexion than white, nor even any individual eminent either in action or fpeculation. No ingenious manufactures amongft them, no arts, no fciences. On the other hand, the moft rude and barbarous of the whites, fuch as the antient Germans, or the prefent Tartars, have ftill fomething eminent about them, in their valour, form of government, or fome other particular. Such a uniform and conftant difference could not happen, in fo many countries and ages, if nature had not made an *original diftinction* betwixt thefe *breeds* of men. Not to mention our colonies, there are Negroe flaves difperfed all over Europe, of which none ever difcovered any fymptoms of ingenuity ; though low people without education will ftart up among us, and diftinguifh themfelves in every profeffion. In Jamaica indeed they talk of one
Negroe

affords no materials which deferve to render it more fo. We know from the an-
tients, who failed a confiderable way round
the coafts, that the inhabitants were in
the fame rude fituation near 2000 years ago
in which they are at prefent ; that is,
they had *nothing of humanity* about them
but the form. This may either be accounted for by fuppofing, that nature has placed
fome infuperable barrier between the na-

Negroe as a man of parts and learning; but, 'tis likely he
is admired for very flender accomplifhments, like a parrot
who fpeaks a few words plainly." Thus Mr. Hume
marks the difference betwixt the feveral fpecies of men,
by their natural capacity or incapacity of exerting in
degree the rational powers, or faculties of the underftanding ; which is the diftinction that Mr. Locke
makes between man and brutes. I diftinguifh man
from man by *the moral fenfe* or moral powers ; and
although a Negroe is found, in Jamaica or elfewhere,
ever fo fenfible and acute ; yet if he is incapable of
moral fenfations, or perceives them only as beafts do
fimple ideas, without the power of combination, in order to ufe (which I verily believe to be the cafe) it is a
mark that diftinguifhes him from the man who feels and
is capable of thefe moral fenfations, who knows their
application and the purpofes of them, as fufficiently, as
the Negroe himfelf is diftinguifhed from the higheft
fpecies of brutes.

tives of this divifion of Africa and the inhabitants of Europe; or that the former, being fo long accuftomed to a favage manner of life, and degenerating from one age to another, at length became altogether incapable of making any progrefs in civility or fcience. It is very *certain* that all the attempts of the Europeans, particularly of the Dutch at the Cape of Good Hope, have been hitherto ineffectual for making the leaft impreffion on thefe favage mortals, or giving them the leaft inclination or even idea of the European manner of life."

All other writers on this fubject agree in thefe relations, or furnifh others fimilar to them : nor have I been able to find one author, by whom I could difcover that there was any fort of plan or fyftem of morality conceived by thefe tribes of Africa, or practifed among them. Their barbarity to their children debafes their nature even below that of brutes. Their cruelty to their aged parents is of a kin to this. They have a religion, it is true: but it is a religion
which

which feems the effect only of outward impreffions, and in which neither the head nor the heart have any concern. They have laws founded on principles, which plainly prove the defective ufe of the *moral fenfe*, as appears in this inftance among the reft. Their Judges are judges and executioners at one and the fame time. When a criminal is condemned by them, the Chief Juftice firft ftrikes him with a club, and then all the reft of the Judges fall upon him, and drub him to death; and neither this, nor any other of their cuftoms, can time make any alteration in, nor precept nor example amend. Indeed, if it were otherwife, it would perhaps be unnatural: for the Ethiopian cannot change his fkin, nor the Leopard his fpots. From this then, my Lord, I infer, that the meafure of thefe beings may be as compleat, as that of any other race of mortals; filling up that fpace in life beyond the bounds of which they are not capable of paffing; differing from other men, not

L   in

in *kind,* but in *fpecies;* and verifying that
unerring truth of Mr. Pope, that

" Order is Heaven's firft law ; and this confeft,
" Some are, and muft be, greater than the reft :"

The application of what has been faid, is,
that the Legiflature, perceiving the *corporeal*
as well as *intellectual* differences of Negroes
from other people, knowing the irreclaim-
able favagenefs of their manners, and of
courfe fuppofing that they were an inferior
race of people, the conclufion was, to follow the commercial genius of this country,
in enacting that they fhould be confidered
and diftinguifhed (as they are) as articles of
its trade and commerce only [*q*].

Thus,

[*q*] There are two cafes referred to in Mr. Hargrave's argument, (p. 52. and p. 54.) which are not only
fully explanatory of the above principles, but fupport
the opinion of the Lord Chancellours, Hardwick and
Talbot; and are in direct proof of the whole of my
argument. The cafes I allude to, are thofe of Butts
and Penny, and Gelly againft Cleve. The firft was
an action of *Trover* for 10 Negroes; and there was a
fpecial verdict, &c. The Court held, that *Negroes being
ufually bought and fold amongft Merchants, and being infidels,* there might be a property in them fufficient to
maintain the action. In the fecond cafe, the Court is
faid

Thus, my Lord, borne on the wings of Fancy, and led by Imagination's wily train, have I ventured in untrodden paths to trefpafs on philofophic ground; to which offence, however, pleading guilty at your Lordfhip's bar, I fubmit to the juftice of the fentence, be your Lordfhip's judgment whatever it may.

But having now difcuffed the *phyfical* motive, which, as it is apprehended, might have occafioned the *civil* exiftence, if I may fo fay, of Negroes in this kingdom; the *political* confideration propofed comes next in the order of enquiry. It muft be obferved, my Lord, that if the caufe already affigned

---

faid to have held, that *Trover* will lie for a Negroe boy, becaufe *Negroes are Heathens*; and therefore a man may have property in them; and the Court without averment will take notice, that they are *Heathens*. Now upon two judicial determinations are the very reafons of my argument held and alledged. *Negroes are infidels: Negroes are Heathens:* of courfe unpoffeffed of thofe religious and moral truths, which the Gofpel impreffes upon all minds capable of receiving them; and therefore the law, regarding the inferior ftate of their nature, has confidered them merely as *property bought and fold among merchants.*

be

be the real caufe, whatever is to be advanced on this head, is ufelefs and fuperfluous. Both caufes cannot be true at one and the fame time. They are meant and muft be received in the alternative; or as the two ftrings of Nimrod's bow, of which if either failed, the other fupplied the want; and of whom Mr. Pope thus fpeaks:

" Bold Nimrod firft the favage chace began,
" A mighty Hunter, and his *game* was *man*."

Now the phyfical motive fuppofes a difference of fpecies among men, and an inferiority of that fpecies in Negroes: whereas the political confideration, on the other hand, infers an univerfal famenefs in human nature; that is to fay, in fact, that Englifhmen are Negroes, and Negroes are Englifhmen, to all *natural* intents and purpofes. For what fignifies the black fkin, and the flat nofe, as the great Baron Montefquieu would infinuate [r]? And yet methinks, if the Baron had had a black fkin, and a flat nofe, the world never would

[r] Vid. his Spirit of Laws, vol. i. p. 341.

have

have had the benefit of his *Efprit des Loix*. Upon this ground then, the queftion that arifes is, what could have given rife to this degradation and debafement of human nature? If thefe our fellow-creatures were inftruments neceffary for the colonizing of America, and to this end compulfory laws were expedient alfo, why were thefe laws not made fuitable and fuited to their nature? Why were Negroes ordained a *mortuum vadum*, inftead of a *vivum vadum*, (fo to fpeak for comparifon fake) to thofe under whofe dominion they came? Might not the laws of villenage have been revived *quoad* them? Might not other laws of flavery have been enacted for their government?

Here is it then that policy, which is the object of my difcovery, muft have intervened. Now the planting of the colonies opening with the 16th century, and confequently commencing nearly with the reign of James I. it appears, that during the reigns of this race of kings, their cultivation

9   tivation

tivation and improvement were fo rapidly had, that, from a ftate of infancy, before the end of the reign of Charles II. they had grown up and increafed to the vigour of manhood. It is in this period of hiftory, therefore, my Lord, that I am to fearch for, and to trace, the caufe of this allotted condition of Negroes: but, as it cannot be expected that I fhould here enter into the particulars of thofe times, fo neither is it neceffary to my purpofe. A fingle incontrovertible obfervation will ferve to reft the whole of what I have to offer on this fubject; and which is this: that from the *alpha* of the reign of James I. to the *omega* of the reign of James II. *to enflave*, was the fixed principle and uniform plan of government. This then at once accounts for the toleration of a meafure, fo inconfiftent with the principles of the conftitution of this country: but the reafon upon which the meafure was grounded is not fo immediately obvious. From things that are more known, things that are lefs known muft be deduced. Now it is a maxim in politics,

politics, that to obtain an end, direct means are not always to be purfued, or rather that *indirect* means are allowed to be prac- tifed; and this will lead me to mention two queftions that have been already ftated. Why were not the laws of villenage en- forced? or why were not other laws of flavery enacted for the government of thefe people? The anfwer is plain; thefe were edged tools, which the complexion of the times would not fuffer the ufe of. Enough was the plan of government expofed, though hid under the cloak of religion. Such a ftep would have left it naked, and without a covering. Policy therefore prevented that which the jealoufy of the people would have forbidden. In vain would have been the argument, that thefe laws were intended for operation in the new world of America. *Ever to begin at the extremes* is a well-known rule in the art of attaining to defpotifm. The more diftant the defign, the deeper laid is the fcheme, and the more fure in its confe- quences. As in the body natural, even fo is it in the body politic. The difeafe

that

that lays hold of the toe, often finds its way to the heart. Gradual encroachments by imperceptible movements are the moft dangerous fymptoms. They call off attention to remedies, and lull fufpicion to fleep. But may all lovers of liberty ever have their eyes open and awake to this defpotic procefs ! He that would tyrannife in America or abroad, awaits only the opportunity of becoming a tyrant at Home ; but thank God, my Lord, the prefent times with us, of all others, give leaft occafion for any apprehenfions of this fort. But to return. Inftead then of that Demon Slavery being called in to prefide over Negroes, Trade, the guardian angel of England, was made the ruler of them. This I attribute to policy ; which, however feemingly more conftitutional, was not lefs favourable to the ruling principle of the Crown. I have already admitted, that to erect corporations, and to grant Letters Patent for the purpofes of trade, are in the Crown its undoubted prerogative ; but, confidering Negroes as human creatures, and upon a level with ourfelves, I fubmit it to

your

your Lordſhip, that the Crown had no right
to make ſlaves of them; whatever the un-
controulable power of an act of parliament
might do: and yet Charles the Second, by
his Charter only to the Duke of York,
enſlaved whole nations of theſe people.
The apology, I apprehend, for this, my
Lord, will be; that neither this Charter,
nor any other Grant, have ever conceived
Negroes in this light and view; as, relation
being thereunto had, will more fully appear [s]. If ſo, my Lord, two things come
out in proof: *preſumptively*, that the
Crown had no right of itſelf to make
ſlaves of Negroes, or it would, in thoſe
days at leaſt, have exerted it; *poſitively*,
by theſe authorities themſelves, that Ne-

[s] See alſo the Aſſiento, or Contract made with the
South Sea Company, for ſupplying the Spaniards with
Negroes by treaty of commerce between Great Britain
and Spain, in the year 1713-14; wherein they are conſidered as dutyable commodities, and named merely as
matters of merchandize; and if thus conceived of at
this time, and on ſo ſolemn an occaſion as a Treaty of
Peace, by what new law or magic is it that they are
now become the ſubjects of the Crown of England, and
intitled to the benefit of the Habeas Corpus?

M   groes

groes are not confidered as flaves under the idea of flavery, but merely as matter of commercial property, and articles of the trade of this country.

If now, my Lord, I have fupported the doctrine which I took upon me to evince, and have fatisfactorily fhewn, that property is the gift of action in this cafe, thereby proving that Mr. Steuart may of courfe legally compel Somerfet to return to the Plantations, I fhall leave its decifion to your Lordfhip, on a quotation of your own words: " It is not my bufinefs to alter the " law, or to make it, but to find the law."

It remains then only to obferve, that if Somerfet is the legal property of Steuart, he, Somerfet, cannot legally be entitled to the writ which he has fued out in aid of relief. The writ of Habeas Corpus is a writ of right given to the fubjects of the Crown of England, for the fecurity of their liberties. If Somerfet can fall under this predicament and defcription, he is open to the benefits

I   that

that may arife therefrom ; but if the law has already fixed the *fiat* of property on him, I apprehend it is a *legal* exception to the writ, and his right is foreclofed thereby.

Having faid thus much, my Lord, on one fide of the queftion, I do not mean to conceal my fentiments on the other. My aim is, to eftablifh the truth : my wifh, that what is right fhould be done. Whatever then is here the refult of my reflections, to obtain the end I propofe, is neceffary to your Lordfhip's information.

When this matter, therefore, was firft in agitation, it ftated itfelf thus generally to my comprehenfion : that as it was a cafe which exifting for two centuries and upwards, and never receiving finally any judicial determination, it had better remain in the fituation it was. It compared itfelf to me with fome cafes of royal prerogative, and of parliamentary privilege, which were excellent in theory, but fubject to inconvenience in practice ; and whofe

beft

beſt and ſafeſt law was that of ſuſpenſe:
but, my Lord, when I found that the caſe
was to be argued, and the judgment of
the Court of King's Bench taken thereupon, my hopes were, that, if it was
poſſible to counteract the law of the land,
the deciſion would be in favour of the
Negroe: for although the knowledge of
their being free might ſpirit them up to
inſurrections in America, yet it would put
a ſtop to their importation here by their
owners, and they would be more uſefully
kept and employed in the colonies to which
they belonged. On the contrary determination too, my Lord, it being ſolemnly
adjudged that Negroes in this country were
not free, I foreſaw that this fatal conſe-
quence might follow: that the trade from
Africa to America would be diverted from
Africa to England; and Negroes, in pro-
ceſs of time, would be ſold in Smithfield
market, as horſes and cattle now are.
Each farmer would have his Negroe to
drive his plough, each manufacturer his
ſlave

flave under his own controul; and America that was conquered in Germany, as was the faying of a very·great man, would become America ruined in England.

A great deal, my Lord, was urged by the learned counfel, of the edicts of France, relative to Negroes: but it does not occur to my memory that this, among the reft, was taken notice of. It may be, that I am mifinformed with refpect to the fact; but I will tell your Lordfhip how I came by it. I have been myfelf, my Lord, a traveller through every province of France, and during my tour I never had opportunity of feeing more than two Noirs (or Blacks) as they are there called; one of which was at Marfeilles, the other at Bourdeaux, the two chief ports of trade with the American colonies of that kingdom. Knowing therefore the intercourfe with, and obferving the fewnefs of thefe people, I was led to enquire into the reafon of it; when I was informed, that there was an abfolute edict of the prefent King of France, prohi-

prohibiting the importation of them into that country, upon this political idea, that otherwise the race of Frenchmen would, in time to come, be changed. Greater much, my Lord, is the reason in this country to apprehend this event. It was in reprefentation, if not in proof, to your Lordfhip, that there were already fifteen thoufand Negroes in England ; and fcarce is there a ftreet in London that does not give many examples of that, which, with much lefs reafon, had alarmed the fears of France. Upon the whole, then, my Lord, let America and England look up to your Lordfhip, as the man qualified to draw the line of propriety between them. To this end, let a Bill originate in the Houfe of Lords, under your Lordfhip's formation : let flavery, fo far as property is fuch in Negroes, be held in America : let the importation of them be prohibited to this country, with fuch other regulations and provifions as your Lordfhip fhall fee fit to take place. Some centuries back, flavery

was

was the law, and flaves the objects of that law, as I obferved before, in this kingdom : but civilization has extinguifhed the exiftence of both. When America fhall be what England is, fome yet undifcovered land will become what America is. In fhort, my Lord, by this act you will preferve the race of Britons from ftain and contamination ; and you will rightly confine a property to thofe colonies, upon whofe profperity and welfare the independent being of this country refts.

SAMUEL ESTWICK.

Portman-Square,
Dec. 10, 1772.

F I N I S.